Katy Cat and Beaky Boo

Lucy Cousins

I am Katy Cat.

Where is my friend Beaky Boo?

I am orange.

What  you, Beaky Boo?

green

lots of colours

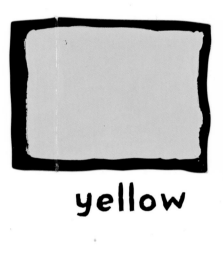

yellow

blue

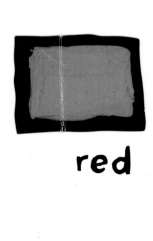

red

I have whiskers.

What do you have, Beaky Boo?

ears

beak

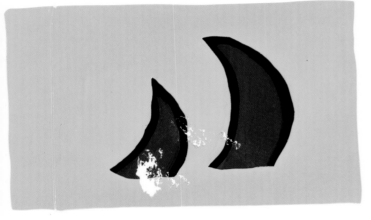

horns

fins

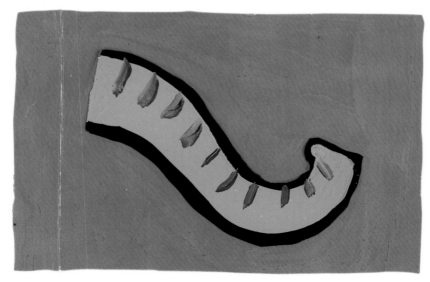

trunk

I am stripey.

Are you stripey or spotty, Beaky Boo?

stripey

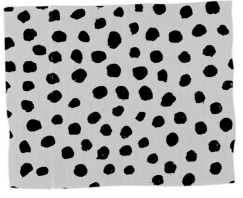

spotty

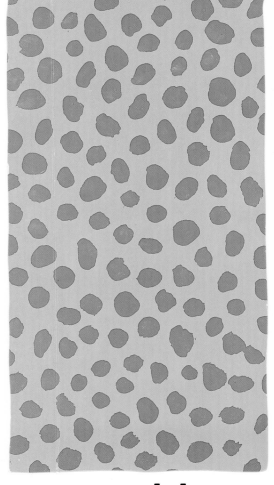

spotty

stripey

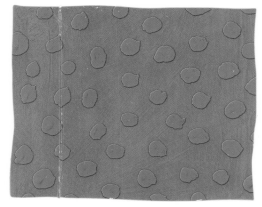

spotty

I can say miaow.

What do you say, Beaky Boo?

cock-a-doodle-doo

moo

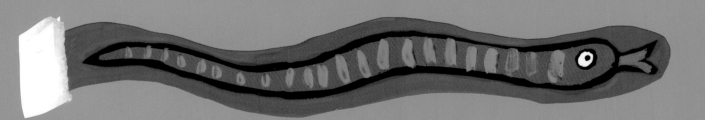

squeak

tweety tweety

I am wearing trousers.

What are you wearing, Beaky Boo?

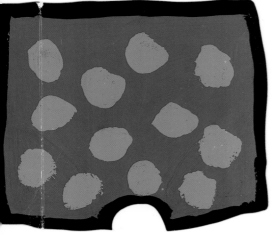

knickers

boots

vest

(4)

hat

I am soft and fluffy.

What are you, Beaky Boo?

prickly

scaly

woolly

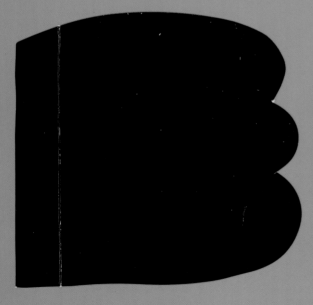

feathery

I like eating fish.

What do you eat, Beaky Boo?

grass

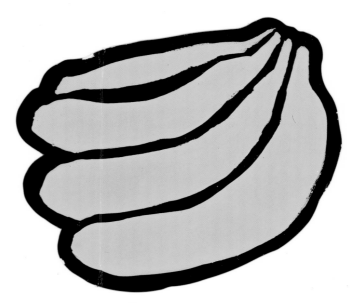

bananas

cheese

sardines

I live in a house.

Where do you live, Beaky Boo?

in a shell

on a rock

in a pouch

in a hive

I have lots of friends